JACOB
and the
STRANGER

BY SALLY DERBY

ILLUSTRATIONS BY LEONID GORE

TICKNOR & FIELDS
Books for Young Readers
New York • 1994

Published by
Ticknor & Fields
Books for Young Readers
A Houghton Mifflin company,
215 Park Avenue South, New York,
New York 10003.
Text copyright © 1994 by Sari E. Miller
Illustrations copyright © 1994 by Leonid Gore
All rights reserved.
For information about permission to reproduce
selections from this book, write to Permissions,
Ticknor & Fields, 215 Park Avenue South,
New York, New York 10003.
Manufactured in the United States of America
Book design by David Saylor
The text of this book is set in 13 pt. Weiss
The illustrations are ink and acrylic,
reproduced as halftone

BP 10 9 8 7 6 5 4 3 2 1

Library of Congress Cataloging-in-Publication Data
Derby, Sally. Jacob and the stranger / by Sally Derby ;
illustrated by Leonid Gore.   p. cm. Summary: When the plant
he is minding for a stranger grows unusual buds, Jacob soon
finds himself the temporary owner of a
houseful of magical cats.
ISBN 0-395-66897-2
[1. Cats—Fiction.
2. Plants—Fiction.
3. Magic—Fiction.]
I. Gore, Leonid, ill. II. Title.
PZ7.D44174Jac 1994
[E]—dc20   93-11022   CIP   AC

For my father, with love and gratitude.

S. D.

For my lovely wife, Nina, for sharing the dreams.

L. G.

A LONG TIME AGO in the old country, in a small house on the edge of the town of Slavda, there lived a young man named Jacob who—according to the people of Slavda—would never amount to much.

"Jacob is kind," a farmer said, as he watched Jacob replace a bird's nest that had fallen from a willow tree. "But he's lazy."

"Jacob is honest," the grocer remarked, opening his cash box to deposit a coin that Jacob had found on the floor of the store and returned to him. "He's honest, but he's lazy."

"Jacob is smart," said the schoolteacher who had taught him as a child, "but he'll never amount to anything. He's too lazy."

"I don't like to work," Jacob would say with a grin and a merry glint in his eyes. "I like to do as I please, to walk through the woods and swim in the brook and lie in the grass watching the clouds."

But now and then, like everyone else, Jacob needed money. When he did, he'd put up a sign that said:

WORK WANTED.
NOT TOO MUCH AND NOT TOO HARD.

And work would come his way. Sometimes a housewife would pay him to run errands. Sometimes the grocer would hire him to dust and straighten the grocery shelves. People were always pleased with Jacob's work and they often asked him to stay on. "No, no," Jacob would say with a laugh. "I never work when I have money in my pocket." Home he would go, and he wouldn't work again until his pockets were empty.

Although the people of Slavda shook their heads, Jacob was happy. All he lacked was a friend to share his pleasures.

"Come take a walk this fine spring day," Jacob would ask his neighbors. But they were all too busy.

"There's too much to do today. Maybe tomorrow," they would answer.

Finally, Jacob quit asking.

One summer day when Jacob's pockets were empty again and he had just put his sign in his yard, he heard slow foot-steps coming along the path to his house. Jacob looked up and saw a stranger in his doorway "Good day," said Jacob. "Welcome to my home."

"Is it you who's looking for work?" asked the stranger.

"I'm afraid it is," said Jacob. "But don't let me keep you standing on the doorstep. Come in and sit down, good sir."

The stranger was tall and thin, with a chin that jutted upward and a reddish nose that drooped like a withered beet. He was dressed in black, but everywhere on his clothes were brightly colored pockets.

"I have a job for you," said the stranger.

"Not too long and not too hard?" asked Jacob.

The stranger laughed. "The easiest job in the world," he assured Jacob. "I find I must take a short trip, and I require a dependable caretaker for my plant." He hooked a thick,

twisted cane over his arm, reached deep into a crimson pocket that Jacob could have sworn was empty, and pulled out a large clay pot that held a slender, branching plant.

Jacob had never seen a plant like this one. It was a soft, silvery shade of green, with many fine hairs feathering out from the stems and leaves. "A fine-looking plant," Jacob said. "By what name is it known?"

"Never mind its name," the stranger said. "All you need to know is that this is a very rare, very valuable plant. What's more, it is about to come into bud. It needs to be set in the sun each morning. It needs a daily watering with a mixture of honey and water. And on no account is it to be taken outside. Do you think you can manage that?"

"For how long?" asked Jacob.

"A week, maybe two," answered the stranger.

"No more than two," Jacob said. "How much will you pay me?"

"A florin a day," said the stranger.

"Agreed," said Jacob.

"There's just one thing more," the stranger said. "You must return to me all that is mine. If you don't, you will rue the day you were born."

"Of course I will return what is yours," said Jacob.

The stranger's mouth curled in what might have been a smile or might have been a sneer. "Remember, all that is mine," he warned, and he turned and strode out of the house. Jacob heard his cane thumping up the path with a queer, hollow sound like the boom of a kettledrum.

After the stranger left, Jacob mixed some water and honey, which he poured carefully on the roots of the plant. Then he set it on the windowsill where the sun could warm it. "Five minutes' work and I've already earned a florin!" Jacob said. "If all jobs were like this, I might not mind working."

The next morning Jacob moved the plant into the morning sun. He noticed that a swollen bud had appeared near the top of the tallest branch. Jacob watched the plant closely

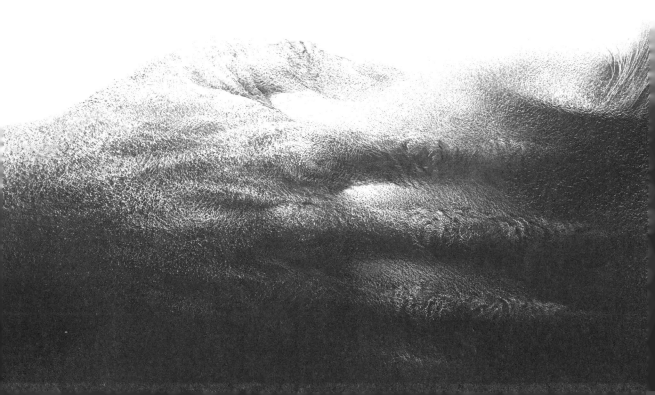

all day. The bud grew bigger and bigger almost by the moment, and from time to time it seemed to dip slightly or sway from side to side.

It was late afternoon, and the golden sun streaming through the window made Jacob feel peaceful and drowsy. Suddenly he heard a soft ripping sound. He moved closer to the plant and watched the bud opening, wider and wider. There, perched in front of the soft green shell, was a tiny black cat .

The cat sat quietly on its

haunches, staring out into the room. It was smaller than a kitten, smaller even than a field mouse, and Jacob realized with a sense of excitement that the tiny beast was not a house cat at all but a black panther. The panther was so small, so perfectly formed that Jacob drew his breath with delight. Jacob stared deep into the panther's green eyes. He had never seen anything so beautiful.

Jacob held out his hand. "Welcome," he said softly. The panther padded slowly and proudly across the back of Jacob's hand, out to his middle finger. Jacob felt a gentle pricking from its tiny claws. The cat paused and looked over its shoulder. Jacob walked carefully around the room, raising and lowering his hand until the cat had absorbed every inch of its new surroundings.

When the panther had seen everything there was to see, it walked onto Jacob's arm, turned to face him, then lay down and began to groom itself. Jacob sat in his rocker, holding his arm very still so the panther would not be disturbed. "How pleasant to have some company," Jacob said. The panther's ears twitched, and the green eyes watched Jacob with a steady gaze.

That night, when Jacob went to bed, he placed the panther beside him on the pillow, and fell asleep running his index finger down the panther's smooth, sleek back.

The next morning Jacob's first thought was for the panther. He placed the small animal on his shoulder and roamed the room, his eyes anxiously sizing up shelves and ledges, tabletops and chairs, searching for a safe spot for the tiny cat. He was still trying to decide what to do when the panther leaped onto the top branch of the stranger's plant. It stepped lightly, jumping from branch to branch, till it found a place where it could stretch out.

It seemed to Jacob that the panther had chosen the perfect place, so he left it there. He ate a little breakfast and watered the plant, then settled down in his rocking chair to watch the play of the sunlight on the panther's glossy coat.

He was so captivated by the cat that hours passed before he noticed there were four new buds on the plant—and signs of movement in each!

That afternoon the buds opened. A lion, a tiger, and two cougars stepped out. The next day eight buds opened, the next, twelve, and by the end of the week more than one hundred tiny animals—lions, tigers, ocelots, jaguars, cougars—were in his care.

The cats made themselves at home. Fortunately, they seemed to require neither food nor water, and at night they curled up comfortably wherever they fancied.

All except the panther. No other panther had appeared, and Jacob was pleased. It made the panther even more special. Each night the black cat would scramble up to sit on Jacob's shoulder. Then Jacob would walk over to his bed, and the panther would settle down on the pillow and allow Jacob to pet it until he fell asleep.

A week passed, a week and a half. The second week ended, and there was no sign of the stranger. Jacob didn't know whether to be glad or sorry. On the one hand, the cats were keeping him busier than he had ever been before. They scaled his rocking chair, picked their way up his curtains, hid

in his slippers. A cougar fell into his soup one evening as it tried to clear the soup bowl in a single bound. Jacob was getting tired of all the work. He tried to keep track of them all, so that he would not incur the stranger's wrath by mistakenly keeping one back. The tiny animals were seldom still and time after time he had to give up. He finally took to going around the room when they were asleep at night, candle in one hand and a pencil in another, counting and recording.

Still, as long as the stranger stayed away, Jacob did not have to say good-bye to the panther, who was becoming

more and more dear to him every day. Jacob always seemed to know what the panther wanted, and often an image would flash into his head—a vision of a waterfall or a jungle clearing, or a still, deep, green pool—as though the panther was sharing a daydream with him.

Now, for the first time in his life, Jacob really wanted money, a large sum of money, that he could offer in exchange for the panther. Lazy Jacob was even willing to work for it. But try as he might, he could think of no way of earning enough. Honest Jacob actually considered stealing the panther, hiding it somewhere when the stranger returned.

When the stranger did return, cold rain was spitting against the windowpane and a chill wind was blowing. Jacob had just finished building a fire in his fireplace, to keep the cats warm, when a rap on the door made him jump. A gusty wind nearly pulled the door from his hands. The stranger entered, brushing raindrops from his hat and clothes, stamping his feet.

"Welcome," said Jacob. "I was beginning to wonder what was detaining you. How was your trip?"

"Successful, quite successful," the old man said, rubbing

his hands together. "How is my plant?"

"See for yourself." Jacob laughed, waving his arm at the roomful of tiny cats.

"Are they all here?" the stranger asked.

"Certainly," said Jacob.

"Let's hope you are telling the truth," the old man said. Cupping his hands in front of his mouth, he gave a high, wailing call that rose, and fell, and rose again. Instantly, the cats scrambled into a line. The stranger snapped his fingers and the line moved forward. Head to tail the small cats came.

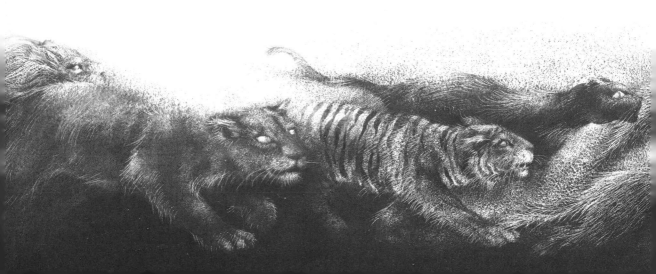

They swarmed up the old man's
trousers, up his coat; they jumped
on his hat and, one by one, they
disappeared into his pockets, each
one heading directly for a particular
pocket. Finally, the last one, with a
flick of its tail, slid into a bright yel-
low pocket.

Jacob sighed sadly. "Well," he
said, "that's that, then."

The old man frowned. "Not quite," he said. "One pocket is empty."

He thrust his hand into the deep, crimson pocket that had held the plant.

Jacob turned to look, and there lay the panther on the pillow of his bed. The tiny cat sat up, but as Jacob stretched out his hand it turned its head away. "He doesn't want to go," Jacob thought. Jacob ran his finger down the panther's glossy back. Then he carried his friend across the room.

The old man reached for the panther, which slowly moved toward the crimson pocket.

"Wait just a minute," said Jacob. "Where is my money?"

The old man laughed. "Money?" he said. "What money?"

"My twenty florins, the ones you agreed to, one for each day that you were away," Jacob said.

"I don't remember any agreement like that," said the old man with a smile. "I don't mind paying you a florin or two for your trouble, but twenty florins is out of the question."

"But you promised!" protested Jacob.

"Promises, what are promises?" said the stranger. "Do you have any contract, something that would stand up in a court of law? You should thank me, young man, for teaching you a valuable lesson. Next time you take on a job, get a contract. Now, I have business to attend to." He turned to the panther. "Hurry, my beauty," he said, snapping his fingers. "In you go." The black cat didn't budge and the old man snapped his fingers again. Then, with a leap, the cat bounded onto Jacob's shoulder.

Now it was Jacob's turn to smile. "I don't think he wants to go," Jacob said.

The old man took a step forward. "You!" he said with a hiss, pointing a quivering finger at Jacob. "You have stolen his heart! I told you that you would rue the day if you didn't return all that is mine."

Raising his cane high, the old man brought it smashing to the floor. With a roar like a thousand winds and a flash like lightning, the cats came streaking out of his pockets. As they came, they grew, bigger and bigger and bigger, until the room was full of growling beasts. They formed a ring around Jacob and, in the circle of eyes surrounding him, he saw reflected a hundred times the dancing flames of the fire in his grate. He shivered. A hot breath on his neck made him tremble and he turned to look.

His friend returned the look. Full-size now, powerful and

proud, the panther stood beside Jacob. Lifting its head, the panther let out a mighty roar, and the other cats backed away. The panther stared at the old man, whose face was white with anger, except for his nose, which was redder than ever. Again the old man raised his cane. "Defy me, will you?" The old man stepped forward. The cat retreated. The stranger took another step and thrust his cane at the panther, but just as he did, Jacob leaped forward and snatched the cane away.

The old man gave an angry cry. "Thief! Robber! Give me back my cane!"

Jacob laughed. "How do I know it's yours?" he asked. "Do you have a certificate of ownership? Something that would stand up in a court of law?"

The old man looked at Jacob. He looked at the circle of cats, and at the panther standing still and watchful next to Jacob. "Be reasonable," he said, calmly. "You have no idea how to control the magic of the cane. In untrained hands its capacity for mischief, for destruction even, is great." He reached for the cane.

"Stop!" Jacob's voice was firm. "It's true I don't know how to control the cane's magic, but I can learn."

Now it was Jacob who raised the cane. Now it was the old man who backed away.

"Gold!" the stranger shouted. "I will give you gold, more than your pockets can hold. Jewels...diamonds, rubies, emeralds. Return my cane and I will give you whatever you desire."

Jacob looked around the small room with its bare floor and rough-hewn furniture. His gaze rested on the fire, and he thought of the glow of rubies. He turned back to the

stranger, stroking the panther with his free hand. "Perhaps we can make a bargain," he said. "I have something you want—the cane. And you have something I want. I'll return the cane to you, and you let the panther stay with me."

"The panther?" asked the old man. "Not the riches, not the jewels?"

"No," said Jacob. "Just the panther."

The room was quiet now, except for the snap and crackle of the fire. The stranger scratched his head, rubbed his nose, clasped his hands behind him, and walked back and forth while Jacob and the cats watched. Finally he stopped and turned to Jacob. "All right," he said. "You have the upper hand, it seems. The panther is yours." Again he reached for the cane.

"Not so fast," said Jacob. "I've learned my lesson. I want you to write out your promise."

Grudgingly, the old man sat down at the table and wrote what Jacob directed: "I hereby relinquish all claim to the black panther in Jacob's possession. I solemnly promise that when my cane is returned to me, I will go away and never bother Jacob or the panther again."

"Just one thing more," said Jacob, still gripping the cane.

"My twenty florins, if you please."

To Jacob's surprise, the old man laughed. "Splendid! Splendid!" he said. "An apt pupil, that's what you are. I pity the next man who tries to cheat you." He reached into a small purple pocket and pulled out a bag of coins. He counted twenty and stacked them on the table. "Now, my friend," he said to Jacob. "May I make one suggestion?" He smiled as he spoke, and for the first time his smile was wholly a smile.

"I'm listening," Jacob said.

"The people of Slavda are going to wonder how you obtained and trained a beast such as this. I'm not trying to trick you now. But I have my own reasons for not wanting people to start wondering where you acquired such a magnificent animal. How would it be if I returned the panther to the size it was before?"

Jacob looked at the panther. He stared deep into the cat's green eyes. "No," he said slowly, "not that size. If too big a cat will raise questions, so will too small a one, and I don't want to have to hide him away. Can you make the panther the size of an everyday sort of cat?"

"Of course I can!" said the old man. "But I'll need my cane."

Jacob hesitated.

"It's all right," said the old man gently. "No more tricks, I promise."

For a minute all was still, then the panther's black head nodded, almost imperceptibly.

Slowly, Jacob held out the cane. The old man took it, and thumped it on the floor, and in a twinkling the cats were transformed once more, racing across the floor and scrambling up into their pockets. All but the panther, which sat silent and proud by Jacob's side. The old man smiled at the panther. "Good-bye, my beauty," he said. Extending the cane, he tapped the panther's head. There was a flash of light that blinded Jacob momentarily, and a cloud of dense smoke filled the room.

When the smoke cleared, the stranger was gone, and for a minute Jacob thought the room was empty. But the sound of a low purr made him turn his head. There on his bed, curled up on the pillow with tail tucked in, lay a small black cat. The cat opened its eyes and looked at Jacob, and the green eyes staring into his were eyes he had seen before. "Welcome home, my friend," said Jacob.

According to the people of Slavda, Jacob never did amount to much. Still, they agreed, a happier man never lived. It did your heart good, they would say, to see him heading out for a walk in the woods, with a grin and a merry glint in his eye and that black cat of his sitting on his shoulder.